ISBN- 978-1-300-66459-8

This is a work of fiction. Names, characters, places, and incidents are either a product of the author's imagination or are used fictitiously, and any resemblance to actual persons, living or dead, business establishments, events, or locales is entirely coincidental.

Some of the quotes in this story are from songs by Manowar™

Printed in the U.S.A

Skratches

book two

The Beginning

Justin Robertson

To my nephew, Alex.

I

2012 (87 years before James discovered the Universe of Olympus.)

Beyond our universe, there is another universe, the universe of Olympus. Within it, there are four planets, and a sun. The sun, is actually the sun God, Apollo, riding his blazing chariot across the sky. The closest planet to Apollo, is Burx.

Burx looks is the burning planet because it is so close to the sun. Next to Burx, is Koalm.

Koalm is the water planet. It's nothing but sea, except for one single mountain that towers over the endless waters. The temple of the Olympian Gods, is perched at the top of the mountain. Beneath the temple, there is the city of Olympus. Next to Koalm, is Tuberok.

Tuberok, is the labyrinth planet. Where the God of the wild, Pan, lives in the depths of the giant maze. The planet was built by Daedalus. Next to Tuberok, is Mechta.

Mechta was a lot like Earth in 2012. Mechta has no oceans, and only a few lakes and rivers. The whole planet was covered with cities, or just one massive city. However it was 50% city, and 50% forest. Forests with trees that are filled with oil. The buildings were very mechanical, most of it was made of metal, and a lot of it was animatronic. Most places had lots of secret passage ways inside of them, walls that would sink into the ground or spin in circles. There was no electricity on Mechta, but they did have generators that ran their refrigerators, and smaller generators that ran their trucks. They didn't have little cars, just trucks. Their trucks had propane lanterns for headlights. Washers and dryers were hand operated. They even had running water. Just, no lightbulbs and no tv.

Juice and Little Darrel were born on the same day to Wayne and Carol. Though he wasn't Little Darrel yet, he was just Darrel because Big Darrel hasn't been born yet.

Dr. Bolt delivered them both. Juice was born first.

The Skratches are all white/Caucasian, with big goofy looking ears, and very big arms.

Wayne is six feet tall. He has long blonde hair, but he was starting to go bald. His arms were the size of couches. He looks like a body builder. He usually wears a black shirt with a flannel coat, jeans, and brown leather boots.

Carol also had long blonde hair. She

stands at five feet and nine inches. She also had arms as big as a set of couches.

Darrel, standing at five feet and nine inches, has always been bald, he preferred it that way. He has a weird eye that had two small pupils side by side, doctors said that it's a gift, it will allow him to see further than the average eye. He had started growing a little bit of peach fuzz on his chin. He always wears a black t-shirt, a pair of cut-off jean shorts, and black combat boots.

Juice was just as tall as Darrel, he was also getting a little bit of peach fuzz on his chin. He usually wears his favorite burnt orange t-shirt, jeans, a belt buckle, and brown leather shoes.

The whole family looked very fit, with very tone, ripped muscles.

Juice and Darrel were both sixteen now, their mom was seven months pregnant with a baby boy.

.

II

"Boys, I'm going to see your Aunt Paula. Frank is gonna be there. Do you guys wanna go?" asked their mom.

"Frank is not exactly the guy we wanna hang out with, Mom. He's kind of a prick," Juice said.

"Yeah I think we would rather stay home," Darrel said.

"Okay, you boys don't have to go. I'll be home in about an hour," she said.

"Okay Mom, bye, I love you," Juice said.

"Love you Mom," Darrel said.

"I love you both very much, see ya in an hour," their Mom walked out the door.

"So, what should we do for an hour?" Juice asked.

"Let's build a fort!" Darrel suggested.

"Inside or outside?"

"What are we? Four? Come on man, we're goin outside."

It was cold out. It was snowing and there was already a foot of snow on the ground.

The Skratches never get cold so they didn't need coats. Even though Wayne wore his flannel jacket, just for looks.

Their house was made of small metal pipes. The pipes were lined up vertically for the walls. The roof was made with diamond plated metal sheeting. There was a lot of mechanical things about the place. Like the dinner table, by operating the crank on the wall, it would come down from the ceiling. The refrigerator was plugged into a giant generator that was just outside the kitchen window. The washer and dryer were also powered by hand cranks.

Juice and Darrel were making a pile of metal scraps and logs for their fort. They used hammers and nails to put it all together. It wasn't your average teenager-built fort. It looked more professional, like a real home for someone to live in. It had everything except for a fridge. It even had a working toilet, and shower.

It took them an hour to build it, and by that time their mom came back home.

"Boys!" she called, "I got Pizza!"

Juice and Darrel sprinted to the house. They dashed into the kitchen and immediately started wolfing down the pizza.

"Save some for your dad, he should be home any time now," Carol said.

In that moment, their dad walked through the door.

"Hi honey! How was work?" Carol asked.

"Could have been better," he replied.

"Are you ever going to tell me what it is that you do out there?" she asked.

"Sorry honey, you may find out someday, but now is not the time," Wayne said.

Carol sighed, "I suppose it's not."

Wayne sat down with Carol and they ate what was left of the pizza, which was just enough for them.

After dinner they played a board game, a unique board game designed by the Goddess Athena. It's like chess but instead of one board, there are four boards stacked up like floors of a hotel. It even had little elevators for the chess pieces to change levels. The goal was to get to the top floor and kill the king chess piece. The roll of a single die determines who controls the team on the top floor. That person must kill all other kings to win.

Wayne got the top floor, Carol was the third floor, Darrel was the second, and Juice got the bottom. Juice was instantly beaten by one of Darrel's rook's. Darrel went up to the third floor and beat his mom, then he killed his dad's king chess piece with his queen.

"Hahaha! I win again!" Darrel bragged.

"You always win!" Juice complained.

"I know!" Darrel said proudly.

"Alright boys, time for bed. You both have school in the morning," Carol said.

Juice and Darrel went upstairs to

their bedroom. The room had a large toy box in one corner, a bookshelf in another corner, and a bunk bed in a third corner.

They didn't go straight to bed. They grabbed a couple of flashlights and played with Legos under a sheet.

"Don't you think we're a little old to be staying up late and playing Legos?" Darrel asked in a whisper.

"Nobody is too old for Legos," Juice whispered.

"Works for me,"

They built an entire city, complete with little trucks. It had a police station, a donut shop, a hospital, a school, a fire station, etc.

Planet Mechta was a lot like Earth in many ways, somehow, they had a lot of the same toys. Legends say that the toys are actually made on Mount Olympus, not on the north pole. However, Santa Clause still delivers the toys, to all of the planets with living things.

Juice and Darrel stayed up till 1:00am, that's when their mom walked in.

"Boys! It's bedtime! Get your butts in bed!" she scolded.

"Sorry Mom," they said at the same time.

They put their city of Legos under the bed. Juice climbed up to the top bunk, and they laid down and closed their eyes.

.

.

.

.

.

.

.

.

III

The next morning, they woke up, got dressed, ate cereal for breakfast, and went to school.

Juice drove his father's vehicle, with Darrel in the back seat. The reason he had to sit in the back seat is because there was a very large four barreled cannon looking thing that took up the entire right side of the cab. If Juice were to push the right button, the right side of the split windshield would fold down, the gun would stick out the window, and a seat would pop up behind the gun. Then Darrel could open the hatch on the ceiling above the seat, then he could sit in the seat, stick his head out the hatch, and fire the cannon, but that wasn't necessary at this time.

Their school was massive, it held over six thousand students and over two hundred teachers. The building was a skyscraper that also had a base that was the same size as a Super Wal-Mart.

Juice and Darrel didn't have any classes together. So they only saw each other during their breaks and lunchtime. They worked on a block schedule, meaning that they would do four classes a day, but a different set of classes for every other day. Today Juice had gym, English, art, and history. Tomorrow he will have math, science, horticulture, and wood shop.

In gym, Juice hung out with his two best friends, Ryan and Tyson.

Ryan had skinnier arms than the other Skratches, but he was probably the most ripped out of all of them. He wore blue jeans and an oversized flannel shirt.

Tyson had a set of goofy buck teeth hanging out over his lower lip, he dressed just like Ryan except for his flannel shirt had the sleeves ripped off of it.

It was a free day that day, so the three of them played basketball against a group of three Itches.

Itches are people with green skin, and pointy-elf-like-ears. They dress like Amazon warriors. They are just a little bit taller than most of the Skratches. Most of them have multiple piercings and war paint on their faces. Every one of them has long, black hair. The males have fangs on their lower teeth that stick out over their upper lips, the females have fangs as well, but they don't stick out.

Juice, Ryan, and Tyson, played against two guys named Max and Dominique, and a girl named Molly.

Max had a big black Mohawk that was perfectly straight up in the air. He wore gold bracelets on both wrists. His ears were pierced with gold studs, and he also had a gold spike through his left eyebrow. He also had red war paint over the left side of his face.

Dominique had dreadlocks, two gold studs on each eyebrow, and a stud through his lower lip. His war paint was blue, it covered his entire face, and part of his upper body.

Molly wore her hair in a single braid that hung down to her lower back. She had large gold hoop earrings on her elf-like ears. She was wearing a dress made of fur, unlike the boys who all wore loin cloths.

Juice and Max stood face to face while Molly threw the ball in the air from in between them. Max jumped higher than Juice and sent the ball to Dominique.

Dominique plowed through everyone and slammed the ball through the net.

Skratches ball - Juice passed it in to Tyson, Tyson passed it to Ryan, and Ryan shot the ball from the three point line. Score!

They played throughout the whole period, Skratches beat the Itches 53 to 38.

Everybody had good sportsmanship. They high-fived at the end of the game.

In English, Juice hung out with his good friend Hammer, another Itch.

Hammer has been one of his best

friends since the first grade. They had to do an art project together and instantly hit it off. Hammer's hair is always parted in the middle, and straight down to his shoulders. He has two gold rings pierced through his left eyebrow, and he wore a black arm band over each bicep.

Juice hung out with Sledge in art, yet another Itch.

Sledge was also one of Juice's best friends from the first grade. Sledge and Hammer are twin brothers, just like Juice and Darrel. Sledge has the same hair do as the genie from Aladdin, with a long patch of hair on his chin that split into two braids with little red beads on the ends. He has a gold nose ring hanging from his nostrils, and he wore an armband on his right arm, over the bicep, just like Hammer.

Juice didn't have any friends in history, except there was a girl he liked, she had long, curly red hair, and big bright green eyes. Her name was Lola. He spent all period just staring at her. Then he got in trouble, the teacher assumed that he was cheating off of her paper. She sent him to the principal's office. Juice tried to explain what he was really doing, but it didn't work. Juice was forced to attend after school detention. Which meant that Darrel would have to wait around for him.

When he finally got out of detention, Darrel was waiting out by the truck, "Jeeze dude, what did you do this time?"

"I was just looking at this girl I like, and the teacher assumed I was cheating off of her," Juice said.

"Did you tell the teacher that? Or the principal?"

"I tried, but they didn't listen."

"That's stupid."

"I know man, I know."

"Oh we'll, at least school is over for today, let's go home."

They didn't say anything on the way home. Their mom was waiting for them outside when they pulled into their driveway.

"Detention again Juice?" asked Carol.

"Yeah, sorry Mom," Juice hung his head.

"You have to stop doing that, one of these days you're gonna get expelled! You're grounded for a month, go straight to your room."

Juice didn't mind, he liked being in his room. He spent his time playing with the Lego city that he and Darrel built the night before, and daydreaming about Lola.

He imagined himself playing basketball. He imagined the same exact game that he played earlier in gym, but this time, he pictured Lola there. After the game, he pictured her walking up to him and kissing him for being such an awesome athlete. "That would never happen in real life," he thought.

As far as Juice knew, Lola hated his guts. Three years ago, they were partners on a science project. They were dissecting a pig fetus together. Juice couldn't handle it. As soon as he started cutting into it, he threw up all over it. Lola refused to be his partner after that. There was no one else for her to pair up with, so both her and Juice got an F on the project. The next day, she screamed at him because her parents grounded her for a month.

Lola hasn't said a word to him since then, but Juice still longed for her. He's had a crush on her since the third grade.

While Juice was adding more buildings to the Lego city, his mind was going a million miles per hour, "Maybe I should just talk to her. What's the worst that could happen? Maybe she forgot about the science project... No, no way she'd forget about that, but maybe she has gotten over it. Still, I should apologize. Hopefully she doesn't slap me."

Juice's mom knocked on the door, "Juice?"

"Yeah Mom?"

"Dinner is ready, you can come out to eat,"

"Okay, I'll be out in a sec," Juice was just about finished with the Eiffel tower that he was building in the center of the Lego city. He put the last little piece on top of the tower and went downstairs to the dinner table.

Gort steaks, mashed potatoes, and corn was for dinner, Juice's favorite meal.

A Gort is a massive mammal that's about the size of two or even three elephants. They stand like a bear. They have hind legs and front legs like a gorilla, a humped back like a grizzly bear, and two heads. One head is like an elk head with long saber-tooth-tiger-like teeth, the other head is shaped more like a cross between a deer and a coyote.

Juice scarfed his food down and was headed back up stairs, when his mom stopped him, "Juice, honey, we need to talk,"

"Okay," he said.

"I will un-ground you and let you join us for a board game, if you can promise me something."

Juice waited.

"Promise me that you won't get in trouble tomorrow?"

"I'll try."

"No, that's not the answer I wanted, I want you to promise me."

"Okay Mom, I promise."

"Good, now help me with the dishes and then we'll play Scrabble."

Juice rinsed and dried the dishes while his mom washed them, then they played a game of Scrabble with the rest of the family. After that, it was time for bed again.

Juice didn't want anymore trouble, so he went straight to bed. Darrel, on the other hand, wouldn't shut up, "Juice, come on man, let's play a game or something, we won't get caught."

"No Darrel, I'm already in enough

trouble as it is. You can stay up if you want, but be quiet, I'm gonna go to sleep."

"Fine, I suppose I'll just go to sleep too. You're no fun."

"Goodnight Darrel."

Darrel sighed, "Goodnight."

IV

The next day didn't go so well for Juice. His first class was math, and the lovely Lola sat in front of him. At least with her in front of him, he could still look at her without getting accused of cheating off of her paper.

He was supposed to be doing equations, but instead, he had decided that it was time to finally tell Lola how he feels, so he wrote her a note, folded it up, and passed it to her.

Unfortunately, just as she took the note from him, the teacher saw what was going on.

"Juice, is that a note? Can I see that Lola?" the teacher took the note from her and took it up to the front of the class, "Let's see what Juice couldn't wait to tell Lola until after class, shall we?"

The teacher opened the note and began reading, "Dear Lola, I'm sorry about the incident with the pig dissecting three years ago, I'm sorry you ended up with an f. I will do anything to make it up to you. Also, I want you to know that I've had a crush on you since the third grade. Will you go out with me? Love, Juice."

Juice was bright red, and so was Lola.

"This is what happens when you pass notes in my class, so don't do it again," the teacher warned.

"Sorry Mrs. H," Juice and Lola apologized at the same time.

"Okay, now get back to work, I need

those worksheets at the end of this class period," said Mrs. H.

Juice completed the worksheet, turned it in, and the bell rang. He went out to the hall and headed towards his locker to get his books for science class. Lola was waiting for him there.

"How dare you embarrass me in front of the whole class! I should smack you!" Lola screamed.

"I'm sorry! I didn't mean for that to happen! I just wanted to ask you out!" Juice exclaimed.

"I wouldn't date you if you were the last man on Earth!" she screamed, and walked away.

Out of frustration, Juice punched his locker door, causing it to cave in. The art teacher from across the hall, watched the whole thing.

"Juice! That's a detention for you mister! You're gonna have to pay for that locker too!" the art teacher scolded.

Juice was even more frustrated now,

he threw his science books at the teacher, and stormed off to the exit.

"Okay, you're expelled then!" the teacher hollered at him as he continued walking down the hall towards the exit.

Once Juice was outside, he realized what he had done. He knew he was going to be in some serious trouble when he gets home.

He sat in his dad's truck, and waited for Darrel to get out of school. After about twenty minutes of waiting, his mom and dad showed up in the parking lot.

His dad walked up and opened his door, "Leave the truck here for Darrel, your coming with us," Wayne said.

"Dad, I can explain, I was just passing a note to this girl I like, and-"

"I don't wanna hear it Juice!" Wayne snapped.

"What happened to your promise? Juice, does anything matter to you? Do you just not care about us? Is that what it is?" Carol asked.

"Mom! Dad! Just listen to me!"

"No, Juice, you can't get out of this one, you're grounded indefinitely," Wayne said.

"Indefinitely? What does that mean?" Juice asked.

"It means that you're grounded until we say otherwise," Carol informed.

They took him home and sent him straight to his room again. Juice was still frustrated, "Why won't they just listen to me?" he thought, "I should just run away."

Juice packed some clothes into a duffle bag, he also packed a couple handfuls of Legos, his piggy bank that had about twenty Mechta dollars in it, and his hunting bow, with a quiver full of arrows. He climbed out of his window, and jumped off of the roof into a tree. He climbed down the tree, and jumped over the fence in the back yard. "Goodbye family," he said, and walked down the street, heading for the forest.

.
.
.
.
.
.
.
.
.
.
.
.
.
.

V

It was still cold outside, snow was on the ground, and icicles were hanging from the snow covered trees. Juice followed a hunting trail a few miles into the forest. The sun was setting, so he stopped to make a fire.

He spent about an hour smacking a couple of rocks together over some dry grass, until finally, a spark landed in the grass and started on fire. He slowly added little sticks and tumbleweeds to the small fire. Soon, he had a roaring bonfire, he curled up next to it and went to sleep.

The next morning he thought about heading back home, but now he was afraid to. He knew he'd be in a world of trouble if he went back, but at the same time, it might be better if he went home now, instead of keeping his family worrying.

He finally decided to go home. Something didn't seem right when he found his way back into city limits. It was quiet, a little too quiet. There wasn't any people walking the streets, no trucks driving around. Something didn't seem right at all.

Juice walked home, but when he got there, his house had been leveled out. It was completely destroyed.

He didn't know what to do, there wasn't a single person or truck in sight. He continued walking around the city. None of the other buildings had any damage, just his house.

He walked to the school, nobody was there either. "Odd, I was pretty sure school was in session today," Juice thought out loud.

He tried to go inside, but all the doors were locked. When he went around to the back of the school, he found multiple buildings that have been torn to pieces. Several houses had been flattened, a few skyscrapers had been tipped over, and a few other buildings were crumbling down. There was a pattern in the carnage, it was a trail.

Juice followed the trail of chaos. He passed many trucks that were either turned on their side or upside down. One truck was sticking out of the side of a skyscraper. Broken glass was everywhere. Juice stepped over many street signs. Still no sign of people, until he heard someone cry out his name.

The voice came from a truck that was turned upside down,"Who's there?" Juice called.

"It's me, your mom, please help me!"

Juice ran around to the other side of the truck, and found his mom trapped under the truck, "Mom!" he shouted, and instantly tried lifting the truck. He almost caused a vain to pop out of his forehead. He pulled so hard that he felt something pop within his eyeballs, and then he temporarily blacked out.

"It's no use, the others went to find help. But they have been gone for over an hour."

It was odd how she was talking just fine, it didn't seem like she was in any pain.

"Mom, are you in any pain?"

"Surprisingly, no. I'm more worried about the baby, I don't think he's gonna make it out of this."

"Well I'm gonna stay here with you. Hopefully the others will be back soon. We'll get this thing off of you."

Juice sat down in the snow, next to his mom.

"Juice, I wanna tell you something, in case I don't make it..."

Juice started getting tears in his eyes, "Mom..."

"Juice, I love you, and if I die, I want you to know that I will always love you. Your unborn baby brother and I will watch over you from Olympus. But there is something else..."

"What Mom?"

"Juice, your father is not who you think he is. He is more than that. Believe it or not, your father is a son of Ares. You're grandma and grandpa are Ares and Aphrodite."

Juice didn't know whether to believe

her or think she wasn't all there because of the truck on top of her. He decided to play along, "So if he's their son, then what does that make you?"

"I'm just a regular everyday Skratch, Ares and Aphrodite are only my in-laws."

"So Dad is a demi-god?"

"No, a demi-god is someone who is born of a God or Goddess, and a mortal."

"Meaning Dad, is a God?"

"Yes, a minor God, he has no special power other than persuasion during war. He can make his opponents change their minds about killing him."

"That's cool, I've always wondered who my grandparents on my dad's side were."

Juice's Mom didn't reply, "Mom?"

.

.

.

.

.

.

VI

Her eyes were wide open, but lifeless.

"Mom! No! You can't die!" Juice started pouring out tears. He sat there next to her and hugged her. He didn't see any reason to leave her there. He would rather die right there with her. He sobbed for several hours.

The rest of the family finally showed up, "Juice! You're alive!" his father exclaimed.

"Yeah, at least one of us is," Juice wiped the tears from his eyes.

Wayne's smile instantly turned into a frown, he looked at his wife, "Carol?" he asked, and then he collapsed. He went straight to his knees and sobbed. Darrel did the same.

"Let's get her out of there, with Juice here, and if all three of us try, we can get the truck off," Wayne said.

The three of them rolled the truck off of her, and flipped it back up on its wheels. Wayne picked her up and carried her off the street, and walked towards the forest. Juice and Darrel followed.

Wayne stopped under a very large Redwood, and set her down. The three of them started digging with their bare hands. As they were digging, Juice asked them what happened to the city, and how Mom ended up under the truck.

"Giants," Wayne told him.

"Giants?" he asked.

"Big ugly red giants, with three eyes," Darrel said.

"Like, real giants?" Juice asked.

"Yes! They were over fifty feet tall!" Wayne said.

"But why'd they attack us? And why now?" Juice asked.

"I don't know, we don't even know where they came from," Wayne said.

They continued to dig a hole big enough for Carol, and laid her to rest. Wayne carved her name and the baby's name in the tree, making it like a headstone for the both of them. They stood there sobbing for hours.

Darrel was giving the carvings in the tree a funny look, "Darrel? That's what you were gonna name him? But my name is Darrel."

"Yes, you're right, I don't know why, but your mother insisted that we had another Darrel. She said that it was important that he was named Darrel."

"Dad?" Juice sniffled.

"Yeah son?"

"Mom told me about your parents, is it true?"

"Yes, I'm sorry we haven't told you all these years..."

"It's okay, do you think that Darrel

and I have any special powers?"

"I don't know, you guys have to find that out on your own. It's hard to say because I'm only a minor God."

"What are you guys talking about?" Darrel asked.

"My mom is Aphrodite, the Goddess of love, and my dad is Ares, the God of war." Wayne explained.

"Oh," Darrel said.

Suddenly, a poof of pink smoke appeared all around them. When the smoke cleared, The Goddess of love appeared in front of them, "Oh great Darrel, I revive you, You will not be unborn, you have a destiny and you must fulfill it. Rise, Oh great one, rise!" she motioned her hands to the sky.

The names that Wayne carved into the tree started glowing, and then the sound of a baby crying came. It was so loud it made their ears ring. The baby appeared in Aphrodite's arms.

Aphrodite handed the baby to

Wayne. Take care of him, he's important," the Goddess turned and disappeared.

"Wait!" Wayne called, but it was too late, she was gone. "Why couldn't she bring Carol back too?"

"I don't know Dad, maybe it has something to do with fate," Juice said.

"Well at least I got my son," Wayne said.

"We should get him out of the cold," Darrel suggested.

"Absolutely, we should build a shelter, and get a fire going," Wayne said.

Juice held the baby, while Darrel started a fire, and Wayne built a small shack up against the tree next to Carol's tree. Darrel got the fire going and helped Wayne with the shack. It was barely big enough for the three of them and the baby to lay down in it.

.

.

.

.

.

VII

They didn't sleep at all, the baby cried all night. They figured the poor little thing wanted food, but they didn't have any. They planned to go find a moothrob that morning.

A moothrob is a cow with long,

floppy ears like that of a hound dog's, and they have tusks like that of an elephant's.

"Juice, can you take Darrel with you and find me some milk? I don't care if you literally have to find a moothrob and milk it, just find some milk please."

"Okay dad, keep that baby warm, we'll be back," Juice said, and he and Darrel went deeper into the woods.

They walked for miles without seeing a single moothrob. After four hours of walking through rivers and over fallen trees, up steep hills and down, they needed a break. Juice still had his bow on him, and with it he shot a couple of falvons out of the sky.

Falvons are large birds, about the size of an eagle. They are bright orange and yellow, with two sets of wings like a dragonfly.

They each forced the raw bird meat down their throats and got a drink from a near by river. Then they decided to head back to their dad, hoping to find a moothrob on their way back.

Luckily, they found one. They slowly walked up to it, but stopped, "Wait, we don't have a bucket, how are we supposed to get milk without a bucket?" Juice realized.

"We'll have to take the whole moothrob with us," Darrel said.

"That thing doesn't have a collar, it's not even tame! How do you suppose we drag it all the way back to camp?" Juice asked.

"Use your belt, buckle it around its neck," Darrel suggested.

Juice took his belt off, and slowly moved towards the moothrob. He just about got the belt over her head, but he scared her away.

Juice and Darrel chased her, luckily, they caught up to her fast. Juice jumped on her back and wrapped his belt around her neck. He buckled it and pulled back on it like reigns on a horse. It worked, the moothrob stopped.

"Hahaha! Well, hop on brother! Let's go!" Juice said proudly.

Darrel hopped on behind Juice, and they rode the moothrob back to camp.

At camp, they didn't like what they saw. The baby was laying on the ground, the fire was out, and their dad was nowhere to be found. The shelter that their dad built was completely torn apart.

They jumped down off of the moothrob and as Juice ran over to pick up the baby, he asked, "What happened here?"

"I'm guessing the giants trashed the place and took Dad with them."

"Or worse..."

"Let's not think about that,"

"Come on, we gotta get this baby to a safer place, maybe we can find a cellar in the city that has heat," Juice said.

"Let's feed him first," Darrel said.

"Right, so what are we gonna do? Just milk the moothrob into our hands or something?" Juice asked.

"I'm not sure if that is a good idea,"

"Well do you have any better ideas?"

"Let the baby suck the milk right from the udder."

"Are you serious?"

"I don't know, I've never fed a baby before, and we don't have a bottle. It's the closest thing to a bottle that we have."

"You have a point," Juice said.

"See?"

Darrel took the baby and kneeled down next to the moothrob's udder. The baby caught on really fast and started taking milk. A few minutes later, the baby stopped, and Juice burped him. He's never burped a baby before, but he's seen someone do it before.

Juice carried the baby while Darrel walked along side of him.

For some reason, the baby made Juice think about Lola. He wished he could marry her and have children with her. He was really hoping that she was okay. He also wondered where his friends from school might be. He was sure his brother Darrel was probably thinking the same thing about his friends. He also knew all about his crush, Daisy. Juice didn't know exactly why he was attracted to her, she's an Itch, Juice didn't think Itches were all that attractive. "Whatever floats his boat," Juice thought.

"So, I was thinking, we should hideout at the supermarket," Darrel suggested.

"Why the supermarket?"

"Because it has everything a baby would ever need, diapers, baby formula, baby clothes, etc."

"Good idea."

They went to the nearest supermarket, MechtaMart, and went inside. Once they were inside, they went and found a hammer, some nails, and some two by fours from the hardware department, and they boarded up the doors. They found some clothes, and some formula for baby Darrel. They found the break room in the back and hung out there. They cooked up some frozen moothrob steaks and ate them in the break room. After that they moved a crib and two beds into the break room and went to sleep.

They stayed there for four more days. Day one, they opened up all of the boxes of Legos and built a bigger city than the one they built at home. Meanwhile, they took turns taking care of baby Darrel.

Day two, they tried building model airplanes and cars, but gave up and ended up riding skateboards down the aisles.

Day three, they played with all kinds of other toys, including musical instruments. Neither one of them have ever been very musical, but they jammed out anyway.

Day four, was a turn for the worst. The ground started shaking.

"Is that a Mechtaquake?" Juice asked.

"I wish it was a Mechtaquake, but it's

probably something much more deadly," Darrel said.

"Like the giants that you and Dad were talking about?"

"I bet so,"

The sound of the giants footsteps were so loud it echoed through the supermarket. The ground shook harder and harder, then suddenly, a giant boot came crashing through the ceiling, *inches* away from where they were standing.

The giant's foot was almost as big as the entire supermarket. When it picked its foot back up, the whole place was trashed.

Now, back out in the cold, they had to find another shelter. They watched the giant walk away. Once the giant was at a safe distance away, they made their move. They jumped over a few fences, and went inside of a mall.

They moved some large vending machines in front of the doors. Juice found a very large ax in one of the hunting stores, and Darrel found a straight sword. The mall was different from a mall on Earth. Most malls on Earth sell mostly clothes and a few gag gifts. This mall sold battle weapons, and hunting gear. Instead of the design your own cell phone cover, it had a forge your own weapon store. The place was abandoned just like all of the other places. They couldn't stay there for long because they didn't have any formula for the baby.

"Let's hang out here for a few hours, and then we have to go somewhere else," Juice said.

"Yeah, we can't take care of our baby brother here," Darrel agreed.

"I just wish I knew what happened to

Dad,"

"Yeah, and I miss Mom too," Darrel started crying.

"I know, me too," Juice cried with him.

A few hours later, baby Darrel started throwing a fit. So they left the mall. They had to find another supermarket somewhere. They walked around the city for several miles. They still didn't see any people, and luckily, no giants. Finally, they found another MechtaMart.

They went inside and did the same thing they did at the first MechtaMart. They boarded up the door, and went to find some baby formula.

They heard voices coming from the back of the store.

"Hello?" Juice called.

The place went silent, "Is anyone here?" he called again.

Two people came out of the back room. It was Ryan and Tyson, Juice's two best friends from gym.

"Ryan! Tyson! It's good to see you guys!" Juice exclaimed.

"Juice! What's goin on?" Ryan asked.

"Well, some bad things have happened,"

"Ya think?" Tyson said.

"Yeah, my Mom died, my Dad disappeared, and now my brother and I have a new baby brother to take care of by ourselves," Juice complained.

"Oh, man, I'm sorry to hear that," Ryan said.

"Yeah, we lost our family too. We were just at the school, and then when the giants came, we ran home, but our family wasn't there," Tyson said.

"We should pack up all of the baby stuff we can get from the shelves and find an abandoned truck, then we should drive it to find everybody," Darrel suggested.

"But what about the giants? They'll kill us," Juice said.

"That's a risk I'm willing to take,"

Darrel said.

"We'll go with ya," Ryan said, nudging Tyson in the ribs with his elbow.

"Yeah," Tyson agreed.

So they did exactly what Darrel planned.

They grabbed a car seat and some other baby supplies from the supermarket and then they went outside and found a truck that seated five people. The truck didn't have a large cannon inside it like Juice and Darrel's dad's truck. They strapped the car seat in the back, and strapped the baby in it. Ryan and Darrel sat with the baby in the back, and Juice and Tyson sat in the front.

They drove through the path of destruction within the city. Until they came to a bridge that had collapsed. There was a way though, if they picked up enough speed to jump over the river.

"Should we jump it?" Juice asked.

"Not with the baby," Darrel said.

"Good call," Juice scratched his

head, then he had another idea, "I'll walk through the river with the baby. Darrel, you jump the truck."

"No, I'm scared of doing stunts like that. I'll walk the baby across, you jump it," Darrel suggested.

"Okay, let's do it," Juice said.

Darrel got out, un-strapped the baby, and walked down to cross through the river. Juice backed up about fifty yards, then he put it in first gear and slammed on the throttle. The truck peeled out and roared down the road. He got it up to about seventy miles per hour by the time he hit the bridge. He cleared the jump by the skin of his teeth. His back tires were inches away from the edge. Darrel met them on the other side, strapped the baby back in the car seat, and climbed back in.

Once they passed the bridge, they were no longer in city limits. They drove down a dirt road through the forest. They had no idea where the giants could be, or the people of Mechta for that matter.

IX

They drove for hours, The road kept getting rougher and rougher. It became so rough that Juice had to slow his speed to about five miles per hour. Pretty soon the road disappeared, and they were driving over small trees, some larger trees that were laid over, and rivers.

They drove until they came to a cliff. They stopped the truck on the edge and got out. At the bottom of the cliff was a very large village with massive wooden cabins. They saw giants roaming around the village. All of the giants were headed into a very large building, much larger than the cabins.

"Looks like an arena of some sort," Juice observed.

"Maybe that's where the people of the city are," Darrel guessed.

"You guys aint gonna do wut I tink y'all is gonna do is ya?" Tyson asked.

"What did you think we were gonna do?" Juice asked.

"Well how else are ya gonna find out

where everybody went?" Tyson asked.

"There's only one way to find out, Tyson, we have to go to the arena," Juice said.

"Arena? Or is it a slaughter house?" Darrel asked.

"Doesn't matter, either way, I'm goin in there. Maybe I'll find Dad," Juice said.

"I ain't goin down dare," Ryan said.

"Me neither," Tyson said.

"Darrel, brother, will you come with me?" Juice asked.

"What about our baby brother? We can't just take him with us. One of us has to stay behind and take care of him," Darrel said.

"Ryan? Tyson? Could you guys take care of our baby brother for us? While we go find out what's going on down there?" Juice asked.

"We don't know nuttin about takin care of babies, sorry Juice, but we don't want that kinda responsibility on our hands," Tyson said.

"Yeah, we ain't any good with babies, the baby might have a better chance of surviving down dare than with me and Tyson," Ryan said.

"So it looks like I'm doin this alone then," Juice said.

"Juice, you don't have to do this, you could just wait it out, maybe if we wait till late at night, and just see what happens," Darrel suggested.

"No, this can't wait, I have to go now," Juice grabbed the hook from the wench on the front end of the truck, and hooked it to his belt, "Wish me luck," he said, and jumped off of the cliff.

They watched in horror as Juice ran towards the massive building in the center of the giant's village.

"Good luck, Juice," Darrel said.

.

.

.

.

.

X

Juice carefully snuck into the large building. Nobody was guarding the door, so he went straight in. Once inside, he found himself in an entrance way to an arena. It looked like an arena for monster trucks. Straight across from him, he could see the dirt pit, in the center of thousands of seats filled with giants. Up above, more giants filled the bleachers near the entrance to the dirt pit.

Juice decided that he wasn't in the best hiding spot, so he went left, under the bleachers.

He found a spot far enough away from the entrance that he wouldn't be seen, and sat down up against the back wall. The giants were chanting up above, "Death! Death! Death!"

One giant stood in the center of the dirt pit, and silenced the crowd. "Welcome Skars, today is a good day for us. Today we will witness our worst enemy in the most terrifying battle of his life. Wayne will finally pay for what he did to our lord, Kronos." Wayne, Juice's dad, was carried out to the pit by two giants. He was in hand cuffs, and there was a giant steel ball attached to his left ankle. "Wayne, welcome to your doom," the giants walked away from Wayne, and went up to sit with the crowd.

A large door opened behind Wayne, revealing the ugliest monster that Juice has ever seen.

The monster was as big as the giants, it had bluish-green skin, and four yellow eyes on its massive bald head. It had tusks hanging out of its slobbering mouth. It only had one hand with two fingers and a thumb, the other hand was just a large metal ball with chains hanging from the wrist.

Wayne didn't have a chance to defend himself. The monster walked right up to him and slammed its giant metal ball into him. Before Wayne could stand back up, the monster picked him up and swallowed him whole. The crowd roared in excitement.

Juice couldn't help himself, he had to cry out, "DAD! NO!!!"

Luckily, the crowd was being so loud, nobody heard him.

Two giants pushed the monster back to where it came from, and then the one giant that was announcing, went back out to the middle, "Ladies and gentlemen,

Wayne is dead, and now we can finally rest, knowing that we have avenged our lord Kronos."

Juice wondered if the Skratches were being held prisoner, if maybe Lola or Daisy were prisoners. He had to continue sneaking around, he had to find the other Skratches and free them if they were in fact, prisoners.

.
.
.
.
.
.
.
.
.
.
.
.
.
.

XI

Juice snuck out of the arena, he began searching for other Skratches and Itches. He searched several empty cabins, but couldn't find anything, not even a clue.

Some of the cabins had giants in them, so he couldn't check those, but he assumed that the people from his city wouldn't be in those cabins. Then he wondered if there might be a basement under the arena.

Unfortunately, before he could get to the arena, the giants started coming out of it. He quickly hid behind a cabin, and slipped away, into the trees.

From the trees he watched as the giants went to their separate homes. Then he saw a girl, a Skratch girl with red hair, come out of the arena. The girl was sneaking around, ducking behind bushes and cabins, the same way Juice was. Juice followed her. He followed her all the way through the village, and into the trees on the other side.

She must have heard him following her, because she turned around and looked right at him.

She almost killed him with her sword, but she quickly realized who it was. "Juice?" she asked.

Juice didn't realize who she was until she had her sword up to his throat and said his name, "Lola!" he exclaimed.

"You're not a prisoner?" Lola asked.

"No, I wasn't even in town when those giants came through."

"Those giants are called Skars, apparently someone named Wayne killed their lord Kronos back in the day, and that's why the Skars attacked us. Now I'm trying to find the others."

"Wayne was my dad."

"Oh my Gods, I'm so sorry."

Juice's eyes began to water, "I don't wanna talk about it right now."

"I know how you feel, both of my parents died when the Skars came through the city, one of the giants stepped on them."

"I'm sorry to hear that, both of my parents are dead too."

"Let's not talk about it now."

"Okay, so are you looking for the others?"

"Yeah, have been for a month now."

"A month? Seriously? You have been sneaking around this village for a month?" Juice asked.

"Yeah," Lola replied.

"Is there a basement under the arena?"

"Already tried there."

"Maybe they're not in the village."

"Or maybe they're all dead."

"I sure hope they're not dead," Juice

said.

"I hope so too, but, I'm starting to lose that hope," Lola said.

"Well, I know you hate me, but if you want, I thought maybe we could look for them together," Juice suggested.

"I don't hate you," Lola defended.

"You don't?" Juice sounded surprised.

"No, sure you've embarrassed me a few times but, that didn't make me hate you."

Juice was relieved, "Sweet," he said.

"Well, I guess we could start looking outside the village," Lola said.

"Okay, let's go."

"Follow me," Lola ordered.

As Juice followed her, he began daydreaming about her. He was trying so hard to refrain from running his fingers through her curly red hair. He tried so hard not to kiss her cheek, or her lips, or even her neck.

He stared at her butt as she walked in

front of him. They walked out to an open, grassy field just outside of the Skars' village.

It was getting dark, so they stopped to make a campfire. Juice gathered the wood, while Lola dug a hole for the fire pit.

They easily got it going, and they sat down, cross legged, in front of it.

"I didn't know your dad was the great warrior who took down Kronos in the early days of Mechta," Lola said.

"I didn't know either, I didn't even know he was a minor God," Juice said.

"They never told you about your grandparents?"

"Not up until right before my mom died."

"Really?"

"Yup."

"Who are your grandparents anyway?" Lola asked.

"Ares and Aphrodite," Juice replied.

"Did your dad have any powers?"

"Only the power to manipulate his opponents minds in battle."

"So like, if someone wanted to kill him, he could make them change their mind?"

"Yeah, that's what my mom told me."

"Cool. What about you, do you have any powers?"

"None that I know of," Juice said sadly.

"Maybe you just haven't found them yet, you're a demi-god aren't you?" Lola asked.

"Yeah, I guess I am," Juice replied.

"I wish I was a demi-god."

"Who we're your parents?"

"Dwayne, and Tammy, they were just everyday normal Skratches."

"Maybe they were keeping a secret just like my parents were."

"Maybe, but I doubt it."

"I never had a clue that my dad was

so special, he acted just like a normal Skratch. He acted just like a normal dad, he took me fishing, hunting, camping, we played catch, he was the best dad anyone could ever ask for."

"Sounds like a good dad, I wish he was my dad. My dad never took me anywhere, he was always busy with work. He hardly ever spent any time with us. My mom didn't really spend anytime with us either. I basically raised my sister by myself since I was eight years old."

"I didn't know you had a sister," Juice said.

"Yeah, she's four years younger than me."

"So she's...12?"

"Yup, she's my favorite person in the whole universe. I hope we find her, I wouldn't know what to do without her."

"What's her name?" Juice asked.

"Lilly," Lola replied.

"We will find her, and my brothers too."

"I thought you only had one brother, Darrel right?"

"Yeah, he was almost my only brother. My mom was pregnant when she died. Thanks to Aphrodite, baby Darrel was born. According to her, he is the chosen one, and for some reason, he had to have the same name as my other brother Darrel. I think it has something to-"

Lola interrupted, "Wait, you've met the Goddess of love?"

"Yeah."

"Amazing, what was she like?"

"Well, besides you," Juice grinned, "She was the most beautiful woman I have ever seen."

Lola blushed, "Um... Sorry I interrupted, please continue your story."

"I don't even remember what I was talking about."

"Something to do with your brothers having the same name."

"Oh yeah, it had something to do with baby Darrel's destiny. I really have no idea though. Right now, my brother is alone with the baby, and he's never had to take care of a baby before. I was with him and the baby for a few days, until I decided to go to the Skar's village. He didn't want to put the baby in danger, so he stayed behind."

"My sister was taken away by one of the Skars. I tried to follow, but the Skar was too fast."

"Well, I promise, I will help you find her."

"You're sweet Juice, I like you." Lola said.

Juice had the cheesiest grin on his face, "I like you too," he said.

Lola looked like she had the same thoughts as Juice, he wondered if she REALLY liked him, or just wanted to be friends. He hoped that wasn't the case. He longed for her. He has daydreamed about her since he first saw her many years ago. This is the first time they actually got along, and the first time they had ever carried on a conversation.

"Juice?" Lola asked.

"Yeah?"

"I'm cold, and tired."

"Me too."

Lola frowned, she seemed like maybe she wanted Juice to cuddle with her, but Juice didn't get the hint. He was way too intimidated by her. She curled up in a ball and closed her eyes. Juice took his shirt off and wrapped it around her, and then he grabbed a stick, and started poking at the fire. He knew he couldn't sleep if he tried, he was too worried about his brothers, his friends from school, and Lola's sister, Lilly. He wondered if things would ever go back to normal, if he'd ever be able to go back to school. He wanted to get up and continue searching, but he couldn't leave Lola behind. He cared more about her than he has ever cared about anyone.

Finally, Juice grew tired. He found some wood, put it in the fire, and then curled up next to Lola and went to sleep.

.
.
.
.
.
.
.
.
.
.
.
.
.
.
.
.
.
.
.
.

XII

Juice was startled awake by the sound of Lola screaming. He sat up really fast and saw Lola being dragged away by a trom.

A trom is an alligator looking thing with a weird fin on its back and a tail that works like a taser.

The reptile had Lola's left foot in its mouth and was dragging her around like a rag doll.

Juice shot up and sprinted toward her, he grabbed his axe and stabbed the trom in the back. The trom let go of her foot, but unfortunately, it grabbed a hold of Juice's left hand. The reptile sliced three marks into his arm with its claws, and twisted itself upside down, ripping Juice's hand all the way off.

"JUICE!!" Lola screamed, as she ran

up, pulled the axe out of the trom's back, and chopped its head off.

Juice was in shock, he didn't feel any pain at all. He sat on the ground and just stared at his missing hand as the blood gushed down his arm.

"Juice! Your hand! Are you okay? We HAVE to find the Stitches to get you fixed up!" Lola was panicking so bad that she couldn’t breathe. She picked him up to his feet, and walked with him. "Hold on, where's your shirt? We need to wrap that up."

They found the shirt by their fire pit. Lola picked it up and wrapped it around his stubbed wrist. She tied it in a knot extremely tight, in order to stop the blood flow. Juice finally started feeling the pain, he tensed up as she pulled the shirt tight. "Sorry, but this will stop the bleeding," she said.

"It's okay," Juice said, holding back the scream he wanted to let out from the pain.

"No it's not okay! This happened because of me! It should have been my foot that got ripped off!"

"Thank the Gods that didn't happen."

"You sacrificed your hand for me, and for that, I owe you. You're my hero Juice."

Even in pain, Juice was able to force a smile. He never thought he'd end up being Lola's hero. It was definitely worth losing his hand.

Lola took him back to the city, back to one of the supermarkets. She found a hook like the one Captain James Hook wears in the Peter Pan movies. She gave Juice some numbing medication, and then with a needle and thread, she sewed the hook to his wrist.

As she was sewing, Juice said, "You're good at that. I can't feel any pain."

"Good," she said as she pulled the last stitch through and tied it, "There you go, I hope you like your new hook."

Juice was checking it out like it was

the coolest thing ever, "Cool," he said.

Lola saw the way he was looking at her, she quickly leaned in and kissed him. She held her lips against his for a very long time.

Juice was shocked, his eyes grew wide at first, but then the magic of the kiss took over and he closed his eyes. He held his hand on her cheek. Her skin was so soft and silky, it made him melt.

They stopped kissing, and they both had big cheesy grins.

"Come on," Lola said, "Let's continue our search."

Suddenly, they could feel the ground shake again. They snuck outside, trying to avoid being seen by a Skar. The problem with that, was the fact that they were surrounded. Over thirty Skars towered over the city in every direction. Each one began destroying the city. One of them was commanding the rest of them, "Clear the whole place out, I don't wanna see a single building left standing."

"Yes Flame," most of them said at the same time.

"Flame must be their leader," Juice said.

"Yeah, well, I think we should get out of here," Lola suggested.

"Good idea," Juice said, "But how do we get passed them?"

"Good question."

The Skars slowly closed in on them, taking down several buildings at a time. The Skars caught sight of Juice and Lola, and they tried throwing pieces of the buildings at them. One of them threw a truck at them. They ducked just in time as the truck spiraled in the air, and landed a foot in front of them. Juice and Lola took off running. They ran right between one of the giant's feet. The Skars threw more trucks, signs, and pieces of the fallen buildings at them, but they dodged all of it and made it into the forest. Another flying truck came crashing into the trees just behind them, the truck was leaking fuel, and somehow it exploded. Juice and Lola dived away from the explosion.

The explosion started a forest fire that was growing rapidly, Juice and Lola had to run as fast as they could, jumping over fallen trees, and zigzagging through everything else, as the fire chased them.

Lola tripped over a stump, and hit her head on a rock. It knocked her out, and she had a gash on her forehead.

"LOLA!!" Juice screamed, and quickly picked her up. He carried her in both arms. He was moving slower now, but still staying ahead of the wildfire.

Finally, he found a lake. He ran with Lola still in his arms, and then waded out in the lake to where he was on his tippy-toes.

The forest blazed all around, the edges of the lake began boiling.

Juice had to swim down with Lola several times in order to avoid falling trees.

Juice stayed in the lake with her for several hours, until the fire finally died. The smoke was so thick he couldn't breath. He thought he was going to die from coughing so much. His arms felt like spaghetti from holding Lola above the water. Once the smoke finally cleared, he carried her back to the shore, and set her down on the rocky beach. He tried and tried to wake her up, but she wouldn't.

.

.

.

.

.

.

.

.

.

.

.

.

.

.

XIII

Finally after slapping her across the face, she woke up. Normally, Juice would never do such a thing, but in this case, he had to, and it worked.

"Lola! You're awake! Thank the Gods!

"What happened?"

"You fell and hit your head on a rock. I carried you out to the lake until the fire died and the smoke cleared."

"How long were we in the lake?"

"I have no idea, judging by the sun coming up, I'd guess it was all night."

Lola kissed him on the lips, "My hero," she said with a smile.

"Well, I don't know what I would do without you Lola. I think I would be lost."

"I would be lost without you too, Juice."

"That means a lot to me."

"Me too. How about we get out of here, we still need to find the others."

"Good idea."

Juice and Lola continued walking through the burned forest, when suddenly, some odd looking monkeys came swinging through the trees. As they came closer, they didn't look like monkeys. They were very strange looking skeletons. With lights mounted in their foreheads, and it looked like they were wearing harnesses. There was four of them, and they all had tribal designs etched into their bones. Their hands had only three fingers, and their forearms were abnormally large, and square shaped.

The skeletons dropped from the trees, and landed in front of Juice and Lola.

"Skratches," one of them said, "I've been looking for you guys. My name is Blade, and these other guys are Machete, Ax, and Razor."

"Why were you looking for us?"

"Well ya see, it's a funny story..."

The skeletons vanished, Juice and Lola began choking. They noticed that their own shadows were choking them.

At that moment, clouds formed in the sky very rapidly. Thunder rolled in, accompanied by the rain. Then lightning flashed across the sky.

Another bolt of lightning hit the ground next to Lola, revealing Razor's body, the Kut was hit by the lightning, and electrocuted to death.

The other skeletons reappeared, Juice and Lola could breathe again.

"Okay! Okay! We're leaving now!" Blade said.

"You're lucky you have the Gods on your side, but someday, Lord Kronos will rise, and the Gods will go down. We Kuts will rule Olympus," Machete said.

The Kuts vanished again.

"So, that was not just a storm?" Juice asked.

"I guess not, I guess the Gods are helping us," Lola replied.

Juice looked up at the sky, "Thank you, Gods of Olympus."

"Amen to that," Lola added.

Juice looked at Lola, "I could really use a nap right now."

"Well, I have no idea how to get out of here. Maybe we could find a cave somewhere, and I'll stand guard while you get some rest," Lola suggested.

They walked back towards the lake where there was a cliff side right next to it. They found a very large cave and went inside. The cave's floor was sandy, so Juice laid down and instantly fell asleep.

He dreamed about his brothers. They were running from a few giants Inside of the arena back at the Skar's village. Big

Darrel kept turning around firing arrows while running backwards. Juice was running from a giant who was holding Juice's axe with his thumb and pointer finger. Little Darrel was hanging on to another's shoulder, stabbing at it frantically with his sword.

Suddenly, the one giant stomped on Big Darrel, the other giant swallowed Little Darrel, and Juice's axe came flying straight at him.

The image of his dream changed. He was with his brothers. They were inside of the giant's stomach. It was dark, and slimy. They were waist deep in stomach fluid. They could tell the giant was walking by the way they were being sloshed around. The giant must have drank something too, because they all just got drenched by a whole bunch of fluid that came out of a tube above. The stomach was much fuller now. They didn't have enough room to breathe any air. Just as they all thought they were going to die, Juice woke up.

As soon as he opened his eyes, he saw Lola looking down at him. She had been trying to wake him up for a long time.

"Finally!" Lola said.

"Was I snoring?" Juice asked.

"No you were flailing around, and screaming."

"Oh, yeah I was having a nightmare."

"I could tell, that's why I woke you up."

"I'm still so tired."

"You can go back to sleep, you haven't been sleeping for very long."

"Okay," Juice said, and he went back to sleep.

He had another dream, a much better dream this time. He was on mount Olympus with Lola, they were riding a Pegasus together. Flying across the sky, touching the clouds as they went by. Lola held on tightly to Juice's upper body as they did barrel rolls and flips.

His wonderful dream was interrupted by Lola nudging him awake, but reality was just as wonderful for him, just because of Lola.

"I found something, you gotta see this!" she exclaimed.

"What is it?"

"Just come look."

Juice slowly stood up, and followed Lola deeper into the cave. They went through a long, windy tunnel, and came to a large door. The door had a large Δ (Daedalus's symbol) on it.

"I haven't figured out how to open it yet."

"I wonder if..." Juice looked around, then he put his hand over the symbol. He tried pushing, but it didn't work. "Daedalus, let us in," he said.

The symbol on the door glowed, and then it opened up like a garage door.

"Whoa!" Lola exclaimed.

"Shall we?" Juice asked, nodding at the door way.

"We shall," Lola agreed.

They couldn't see anything passed the doorway, it was pitch black. They slowly walked in. They walked through darkness for a long time.

"Juice, I'm scared, I can't see you, are you still there?"

"I'm here, grab my hand," Juice said, as he fondled around trying to find her hand. They finally found each other's hands and held on. They continued walking through the darkness. Suddenly a loud screech echoed through the place.

It sounded like somebody farted through their nose, sneezed, and then screamed like a girl, all at the same time.

Juice and Lola froze.

"What was that?" Lola asked in a whisper.

"I don't know," Juice whispered back.

"I'm not sure if I even *wanna* know.

"Me neither, but I have a bad feeling that we're gonna find out whether we like it or not."

"Let's go back, I want to get out of here." Lola panicked.

"Okay," Juice was also getting really freaked out. He's never been a big fan of the dark. He used to have to have a night light in his room clear up until he was thirteen years old.

Juice and Lola were walking really fast, they would have been running if only they could see. They walked for a really long time, it seemed like they should have came to the door shortly after they turned around but they never found it.

"Where did the door go?" Juice asked.

"I don't know, I think we passed it!"

They turned around and walked in the other direction again, but they still couldn't find the door.

The screeching sound kept getting louder and louder.

Juice and Lola stumbled over a pile of boxes. Inside the boxes were some rocks, bricks, a couple of putty knives and some flashlights. They couldn't really see the stuff until they felt the flashlights and turned them on.

"I thought the labyrinth was on Tuberok," Juice said.

"It is, but I think he made a smaller one here, as a model."

"Makes sense."

They heard the screech once more. Juice turned around with his flashlight. The tunnel they were in was sparkling with several crystals and other jewels, but horrifyingly, the thing that was making the screeches, was standing on four legs, right behind him.

The creature stood up right, like a human, but with four legs and four arms. Each limb had a hand with two fingers and a thumb. On the palms of each of the upper hands, had little slits on them. It screeched again, revealing that the sounds we coming from the slits on its palms. The slits were actually mouths. It didn't have a mouth on its head, but it had huge eyeballs popping out of its head, and a long elephant like nose. This thing was around six feet tall, and had neon blue skin. The only hair on its body was on its forearms. The rest of it looked very slimy, and gross.

The blue monster grabbed Juice with all four of its arms. Neither one of them had weapons. Lola tried to attack the monster with her fists, but it wasn't helping.

Juice could feel the mouths on its palms, biting into his skin, and sucking the blood out. Juice squirmed, and pried, but he couldn't break free. Soon he felt his energy drain, he grew weak, and started getting a serious headache.

Lola continued punching and kicking the monster, but it still wasn't doing any damage.

Juice was blacked out now, he had lost way too much blood. The monster let go of him, he fell to the floor, unconscious.

XIV

Then the monster turned its attention towards Lola, she quickly turned her flashlight off, and ran in the other direction. She expected the monster to catch up to her, but it didn't. She couldn't hear it following her, so she stopped. The monster didn't follow. She worried about Juice, so she turned back again and walked back towards him. As she walked, she was able to hear the monster screeching again. She turned her flashlight back on, and there it was. It leaped at her, and she turned the light off again. She thought it would have tackled her, but it didn't.

"The light," she thought to herself, "It won't attack me without the light, but how am I supposed to find Juice without it?" she got down on her hands and knees, and crawled around on the floor, hoping she would find Juice. As she crawled she accidentally put her hands on the blue monster's feet, the monster jumped back and scurried away.

She stood back up, flashed her light around the room really quickly, and shut it off. She saw Juice as she flashed the light, and she walked in his general direction. As she walked, she continued flashing her light, on and off, really quickly. When she reached his body, she tried gently kicking him, at first, then she started kicking harder. Juice didn't move. Lola sat down next to him, and shook him. She smacked him several times, and he finally woke up.

"Where's the monster?!" he yelled with a whisper.

"It's gone, it won't hurt us as long as we keep the flashlights off."

"Wow, how did you figure that out?"

"I just did."

"Oh okay, well how about that? You saved *my* life."

"Yes I did, now I don't feel like I owe you anything."

"You never owed me anything in the

first place."

"I know, but, I just feel better now."

"Okay. So, did you happen to find a way outta here while I was unconscious?"

"Afraid not."

Juice tried to stand up, but he had to have Lola help him. They held hands again and continued searching for the door. They saw an orange glow in the distance, "That's it!" Juice shouted, pointing at the orange light.

They ran towards the glow, and sure enough it was a door with Daedalus' symbol on it.

It opened up as soon as Juice put his hands on it, but the other side did not look familiar at all.

The door led to a well lit room, full of boxes and desks with computers on them. It was a very small room, so Juice and Lola didn't bother going inside. They closed the door so that the light wouldn't attract the blue monster.

They turned around and walked back

into the darkness, quickly flashing their lights around. They found another door, and went through it. It took them to a familiar cave entrance, but where the lake should have been, was a large body of boiling hot lava. A volcano was on the other side, pouring the lava down into the large lake of lava below. Dragons were flying around up above.

"Where are we?" Lola asked.

"I have no idea, I've never seen this place before."

One of the dragons swooped down and landed in front of them. Juice and Lola ran back to the door, but the door was gone. They were trapped in the cave with the dragon.

The dragon was red with a black belly, black claws, and black spikes all over it's back. It wasn't very big, about the size of a kangaroo.

Juice ran up to the dragon, "Yaw! Yaw! Get out of here!" he shouted as he threw his arms up in the air.

Angrily, the dragon took a deep breath. Smoke rolled off of its tongue as it breathed. Then it started coughing.

Juice and Lola gave it a funny look. Slowly, Juice approached it. He walked around to it's backside and smacked it on the back.

The Dragon burped and let out a stream of fire.

Surprised, the dragon looked at Juice, and bowed to him. Juice pet him on the head, it shoved it's nose under him, and threw him onto its back.

Lola stood there in total shock and awe. She couldn't believe her eyes. The dragon motioned for her to climb on with Juice.

"He likes us, come on Lola, let's go for a ride!" Juice said, holding his hand out to her.

Lola still looked shocked as she climbed on the dragon's back, behind Juice. She held on tightly to his waist and the dragon turned to face the volcano. It took off into the air from out of the cave, it flew over top of the volcano and over several other volcanoes. They flew up into the clouds just like in Juice's dream with the Pegasus. Then when they came back down, the view down below was spectacular. It was a tropical paradise with many palm trees and several lakes and ponds with sandy beaches…

Suddenly, Lola vanished, the Dragon vanished. They were no longer in the air. They were back in the lake, Lola was still unconscious in his arms as he was holding her above the water.

The whole thing was a hallucination. Something from smoke rolling off of the trees caused Juice to hallucinate.

.

.

.

.

.

XV

After the smoke cleared he repeated everything he did before, but this time Lola didn't wake up.

He had a déjà vu with the Kuts, but the whole time, Lola was still unconscious. After the Kuts left, he took her into the cave and looked for the door with the mark of Daedalus on it, but the door wasn't there. He closed his eyes and hoped he would see the dragon and the volcanoes when he turned around, he hoped that Lola would be on its back and telling Juice to hop on with her. Unfortunately, when he opened his eyes, everything stayed the same. He continued trying to wake her up...........

.

.

.

.

.

.

.

.

.

.

.

.

.

.

.

.

.

16 years later

Lola never woke up. Juice stayed in the cave with her the whole time. The trees had grown back, and he had cut some of them down to build some furniture for the cave. Shortly after he found the cave, he went out and killed a gort with a bow and arrow that he made. It was a left handed bow, because it was easier for him to pull the string back with his hook. Normally he would use a right handed bow, but he couldn't with his hook.

He chopped up some gort steaks and force fed them to Lola everyday, three times a day. He didn't have anyway of keeping the meat cold, so he had to hunt everyday, most days, he went without eating. Instead he gave all of his food to

Lola.

The gash on her head was gone, she still looked beautiful even though she really looked like a mess. Juice thought she woke up once, but he must have been dreaming because she was still in the bed that he made out of gort fur, and a few trees. He didn't make a bed for himself, he considered himself her boyfriend, so he slept in the bed with her every night. Plus, it was the best way to keep her safe while he slept.

Now, sixteen years later, he woke up next to her. Her body seemed colder than normal, and she didn't seem to be breathing. Juice panicked, he gave her CPR, but nothing happened. She had no pulse.

Juice threw a fit, "LOLA!!! WHY? Why Lola! Aphrodite, why can't I have my true love? Why did she have to die!?"

Juice collapsed, and sobbed. He was crying so bad that he couldn't breathe.

The girl he had a crush on for several

years, the girl who he finally made fall in love with him, could only love him back for a day and a half, and then she went into coma, and never came out.

Juice didn't hunt, he didn't fish, he didn't even move. He held Lola in his arms and cried for three days, nonstop. Juice wanted to die.

Finally, he decided it was time to bury her. He didn't have his axe anymore, so instead of burying her, he gave her the Viking burial. He put her on a raft, lit it on fire and pushed her out to the middle of the lake. He sobbed the entire time.

.

.

.

.

.

.

.

.

.

.

XVII

Juice finally decided that he need to eat, so he grabbed his bow and went out hunting. That's when he saw his brothers.

Baby Darrel, now sixteen years old, was walking in front of his older brother Darrel, and hundreds of other Skratches and Itches. Juice knew most of them from school. Ryan and Tyson were there, Max and Dominique were there, Sledge, Hammer, Molly, Elizabeth (Molly‘s sister), Juice’s cousins Frank and Tank, etc. He was sure he saw Lola’s sister, Lilly there too, and his twin brother’s crush, Daisy.

Juice walked right up to the crowd, “Darrel!” he exclaimed.

“Juice!” older Darrel called back.

“Is that our baby brother in front of you?” Juice asked.

“Yeah, we call him Big Darrel, because the Gods say he is important, he is the chosen one,” older Darrel said.

“So if he’s Big Darrel, then you’re…”

“Little Darrel,”

“But you’re like, four feet taller than he is,” Juice argued.

“I know, funny huh?” Little Darrel chuckled.

Big Darrel is about the size of an

average human. He looks a little bit like Juice but with no facial hair and a small scar on his upper lip. He was wearing nothing but a pair of blue jeans and boots. He was carrying a quiver, and a sword on his back, and a compound bow in his hand. He also had a tattoo of crosshairs on his right shoulder.

"Anyway, Juice, Big Darrel is leading us into battle, and where have you been all this time? You don't look very good," Little Darrel said.

"I've been with Lola…" Juice started tearing up.

"Lola? My sister?" A young girl asked.

"Are you Lilly?" Juice asked the girl.

"Yes," she replied.

"I'm sorry Lilly, but…she…she…" Juice burst into tears, he couldn't say the words.

"She didn't make it, did she…" Lilly assumed.

"I'm sorry Lilly, she didn't."

Lilly sat down on the ground and began sobbing.

"Juice, come fight with us, get your mind off of things. Fight for glory, with a heart of steel. Right now you make it look like your heart is made of jelly," Little Darrel said.

"My heart *is* jelly, it's broken," Juice said.

Little Darrel sighed, "Juice, come on man, be our brother! Fight by our side! Till the blood on your hand is the blood of a king, and till the blood on your sword is the blood of a king! JUICE! Brother, let's do this," Darrel preached.

"Okay! I'm coming," Juice said.

The Itches were on horses, the Skratches were on foot.

Juice walked along side of Ryan and Tyson.

"Wait till ya see where we is headed," Tyson said to Juice.

"Why's that?" Juice asked.

"Me and Tyson builded us a helimacopter," Ryan said with excitement.

"Why does that scare me?" Juice asked.

"Hoo hoo! It's fun!" Ryan laughed.

"Yeah, fun for you, I personally don't really wanna play," Juice said.

"Sissy," Tyson teased.

"It's actually gonna help us big time when we face dem dare Skars over dares," Ryan said.

"Yeah, so what has happened all this time that I have been gone?" Juice asked.

"Well, we rebuilt some of the houses in our city. The Itches built some tree houses in the forest. We found most of these people in their hidden fallout shelters. Darrel stayed in one of the tree houses with baby Darrel until he was old enough to fight. He's been archery training since he was four years old. He's probably the best archer we know," Ryan said.

"What happened to Lola? If you

don't mind me asking," Tyson asked.

"I found her in the Skar's village. We were in love for one night and then the Skars hunted us. They chased us into the forest, and we were suddenly surrounded by fire. Lola hit her head, and I took her into a nearby cave. I had no idea I was in there with her for sixteen years. The worst of it is, she never woke up, instead, she just died…" Juice started choking up again.

"We thought you were dead," Tyson said.

"I'm sorry guys, but I had to take care of Lola. I loved her, I *still* love her. I just wish I could have saved her," Juice broke down again.

Lilly was in front of them, she turned around to face them and started walking backwards, "Juice, you are a hero, don't feel bad that you couldn't save my sister. It's not your fault. Right now, she's watching over you. She's watching over all of us. And she still loves you."

"Thanks Lilly," Juice said.

"No problem, I'm good at making people feel better, it's what I do," Lilly said.

After miles and miles of walking, they finally came to the city, it was completely demolished. Grass grew through all the streets, making all the streets disappear. There were only a few buildings that were rebuilt.

A large helicopter with two propellers on top was perched on top of a tall building off in the distance. There were several guns mounted all over it.

"Well, Juice, that's our ride, what do you think?" Ryan asked.

"That looks pretty awesome," Juice complimented.

"Thanks, we spent two years building it," Tyson said.

"You guys never had anymore trouble with the Skars?" Juice asked.

"Surprisingly, no, but I think it's

because we spent most of our time in the fall out shelters," Ryan said.

"True," Juice agreed.

"You sure you doewanna ride dat dare helimacopter?" Tyson asked.

"I'm sure, thanks," Juice said.

"Alright, you're missin out though," Tyson said.

"I know, I'll be okay," Juice said.

"Okay buddy. We're gonna go for a ride. Hopefully we shoot some Skars with that thing. See you after the battle Juice," Ryan said.

"Love ya buddy," Tyson said to Juice.

"Love you too man," Juice said back.

"Me too Juice, I love ya dude," Ryan said.

The three of them hugged, and then Ryan and Tyson climbed aboard the helicopter.

Big Darrel turned around, "This is it everybody, we're headed straight for the

Skars' village. Are we ready?"

"YEAH!!" the crowd shouted.

"Hold on, I don't have my axe," Juice said.

"Here, give me your bow, and you can have my axe, it was actually Lola's axe," Lilly said.

"Thanks Lilly, that means a lot to me," Juice said.

The Darrel brothers hugged Juice, "Juice if we don't make it out of this, let it be known that we all love each other," Big Darrel said.

"Of course," Juice agreed.

"Absolutely," Little Darrel said.

"Let's go kick their sorry butts off of this planet!" Big Darrel exclaimed.

.
.
.
.
.
.
.
.

XVIII

The sun was setting in the Skar's village. They were all in their cabins. Ryan and Tyson fired several rounds from their helicopter at the cabins, but it didn't do much damage. Hundreds of Skars came out, ready to fight.

First, each of the Itches fired arrows at them, each arrow stuck into one of the Skars, but this only made them even more angry.

The Skars charged at them. The Skratches and the Itches were very careful not to get stepped on.

Several bullets continued to fly from Ryan and Tyson's helicopter. They killed five or six Skars, but one of them reached up and swatted them into a tree. The helicopter exploded. There was no telling whether Ryan and Tyson survived or not.

Juice climbed up the back of one of the giants and chopped at its head with his axe. The giant reached back and picked him up. Then it threw him into a cabin several yards away. Juice went through a wall, and landed on a table inside the cabin. He was okay though, he went back outside and continued fighting.

Max and Dominique were both firing arrows simultaneously at a giant's head, but it was only making the giant angry.

The Darrel brothers and Lilly were firing their arrows all at once at another giant. It was Big Darrel's arrow that went through the giant's heart, and killed it.

Juice was helping Sledge and Hammer with another Skar. Juice was chopping the giant's toes off, while Sledge was hacking at its Achilles tendons. They made the giant fall to his knees, and then Hammer climbed up and stabbed it in the heart with his sword.

Molly and Elizabeth were taking on one of the only female Skars. They did the same thing that Juice, Hammer, and Sledge just did.

Little Darrel climbed on another one's back, but before he could do anything, the Skar grabbed him. With it's massive fingers, it ripped both of Little Darrel's legs off, and his right hand.

The fight continued on and on, until the only Skratches left were Juice, the Darrel brothers, Ryan, Tyson, and Juice's cousins, Frank, and Tank. The only Itches left were, Sledge, Hammer, Molly, and Elizabeth. Juice tried to save Lilly, but a giant stepped on her before he could get to her. Max and Dominique were crushed by a massive tree that was thrown at them by one of the Skars. Nobody knew what really happened to the rest of them.

Big Darrel got Little Darrel out of there, he told Juice that he was gonna get him fixed up, and then they would be back. Everyone else, retreated.

Or they thought they retreated, but they couldn't get away. The Skars threw them all into separate prisons, down underneath a graveyard beneath the Skar cemetery. It was a tomb, and everybody was trapped, and separated, all in separate areas.

.

.

The prison with Juice, Ryan, and Tyson

The three of them were trapped in a large room, filled with Skar bones. Thousands upon thousands of bones were piled up in the room. Juice, Ryan and Tyson were stumbling around trying to find a way out.

Ryan found an old scroll buried under the bones. He picked it up and unrolled it.

The scroll looked like this:

Βυριεδ δεεπ ιν θε δεπθσ οφ βονε
ονε μυστ φινδ α λεϖερ βελοω
δοων δοων δοων
δεεπερ βελοω
τακε θε κεψ ανδ υσε ιτ ωισελψ

Without knowing how, Ryan translated it:

"Buried deep in the depths of bone
One must find a lever below

Down down down,
Deeper below,
Take the key, and use it wisely."

"How'd you read that?" Tyson asked.

"Um… I don't know," Ryan said.

Juice started digging through the bones. Ryan and Tyson joined in to help him. They found the lever and pulled, causing the whole floor to begin sinking. They went down about twenty feet, and stopped. A door appeared on the wall at the bottom. It opened, and they found themselves in a large room with a giant chess board, complete with giant chess pieces.

A white pawn moved by itself and knocked over a black pawn. The black pawn rolled out of the way on its own.

They waited for something else to happen, but nothing did.

"I think we have to move the

pieces," Juice said.

"So we're the black pieces ya think?" Tyson asked.

"Yeah, help me move this pawn," Juice said.

All three of them pushed the black pawn two spaces forward. Another white pawn moved next to it. They pushed another pawn in front of that one, which freed up their rook. Another white pawn moved, and they pushed the rook into one of them. Slowly, the white pawn that they pushed their rook into, moved off of the board. Oddly it ended up being a fairly easy game for them, they killed the white king with their queen. However, the king didn't move off of the board. Instead, it came to life.

.

.

.

.

.

The king grew a set of arms and legs

and attacked them. It kicked Tyson in the face, and knocked him over.

Ryan ran up to it, jumped, and tried drop-kicking it in the mid-section, but the king caught his foot and threw him backwards. Ryan went flying into the other chess pieces that were on the sidelines. Ryan tried getting back on the board, but there was a force field preventing him to do so.

Juice took more of a wrestling approach, and tried going in for a single leg take down. He got the king on its back, but the king rolled over and stood back up before Juice could get a hold of it.

Tyson was back up, and he punched the king in the back of the head as it was going to attack Juice. The king turned around, picked Tyson up by his flannel vest, and threw him off of the board. Neither Ryan or Tyson could get back on.

It was all up to Juice. Juice did a *double* leg take down this time, and quickly moved up to do an arm-bar. The king tapped out. It should have lost by submission, but the king stayed on the board and continued to attack. Finally, Juice picked the king up, fireman's carry style, and threw it off of the board. Ryan and Tyson climbed back up on the board to celebrate Juice's victory, but their little party was cut short by the rest of the white chess pieces. All of the pieces came to life, and closed in on them. Just before Juice, Ryan, and Tyson could make a move, the black pieces came from behind and attack the whites. The three Skratches snuck off of the board, and watched from the sidelines.

The battle between the chess pieces was short lived. The black team defeated the white, and the white pieces crumbled. All of the black pieces went back to their original positions. Juice, Ryan, and Tyson stepped back onto the board. A key fell from the ceiling and the black chess pieces disappeared.

.
.
.
.
.
.
.
.

XXI

The three of them noticed a bunch of keyholes on each of the black and white squares on the empty chess board.

"Use the key wisely," Ryan said.

"So, which keyhole do we use the key on?" Juice asked.

"I would guess that we try the ones

on the black squares, because the black team was on our side," Tyson replied.

"Okay, but which black square?" Ryan asked.

"The middle one," Juice guessed.

"Are you sure?" Tyson asked.

"No, but it's a black square, dead center," Juice replied.

"What if you're wrong?" Ryan asked.

"Only one way to find out," Juice said.

Ryan picked the key up, and put it in the keyhole on the black square in the center of the chess board. He turned the key, and pulled the square out of its hole. Under the square, Ryan found another scroll.

It was written in Greek, and Ryan translated it: "Good choice, but we are sorry, you may not leave our prison. Sincerely, the Skars."

"What!?" Ryan exclaimed.

"I was wondering what the deal with

all the puzzles was, shoulda known that we wouldn't be able to get out," Tyson said.

"No, we'll get out, we *have* to," Juice said, and he took the key out of the black square, and put it in a randomly selected white square. He pulled the white square out, and suddenly the whole place started shaking and crumbling.

.
.
.
.
.
.
.
.
.
.
.
.
.
.
.

.
.
.

XXII

A large crack ran through the floor, and the giant chess board. It continued to run up the walls, and across the ceiling. Ryan and Tyson were on one side, and Juice was on the other as the crack spread open wider and wider, revealing hot lava down below.

Juice couldn't reach them. The building continued to shake and crumble, until the entire ceiling caved in. Juice was still alive, but he couldn't see his friends anymore.

"Guys!?" he called, "GUYS!!" he called louder, but there was no answer. "RYAN!! TYSON!!!" he screamed, but still there was silence.

Suddenly, he heard a voice, "Juice?"

"Ryan? Tyson?" he asked.

"No, it's me, Tank."

"Tank? Where are you?"

"On the other side of this wall."

Juice saw a light flashing through a crack, he went over to it and peeked through it. He saw Tank on the other side.

"It's good to see you Juice, have you seen the others?"

"Well, I was with Ryan and Tyson, but I lost them."

"Oh no, that's not good. I have Frank with me. Stand back, I'm gonna kick this wall down."

Juice stood back, and Tank booted the wall. The wall gave way, and Tank made the hole big enough for him and Frank to fit through it.

Frank didn't say anything, but he

was so happy, he hugged Juice.

Juice would have never expected a hug from Frank, but it was nice for a change. “It’s good to see you guys,” Juice said.

“What about Ryan and Tyson? We should go find them,” Tank suggested.

“Well, we can’t get to them from here, they’re over there,” Juice pointed to the destruction from across the river of lava.

“There has to be a way to get across,” Tank said.

Without saying anything, Frank picked up a support beam and dropped it so that the far end landed on the other side of the lava river.

“Smart thinking,” Juice said, and the three of them carefully crossed over the beam.

They all started moving big chunks of stonewall and support beams. They could hear Ryan and Tyson on the other side of the destruction. They finally cleared enough stuff to where they could see Ryan and Tyson stuck under the pile of rubble.

"We're stuckded!" Ryan said with a chuckle.

"Hey! Frank and Tank! Where did you guys come from?" Tyson asked.

As the other three got them out of the rubble, they explained how Tank found Juice.

"There is a way out of here, but it's kind of a long fall," Tank said.

"Well that doesn't sound like a very good escape plan," Tyson said.

"Yeah but, there is a lake down below," Tank said.

"Oh, well in that case, I'd be willing to try it," Tyson said.

"We have to go back across the bridge that Frank made, and through the hole that I made," Tank said.

"Okay, let's go!" Juice said, and all five of them went to the opening in the side of a cliff. One by one, they jumped down, into the lake.

.
.
.
.
.
.
.
.
.
.
.
.
.
.
.
.

“Wait, how did Tyson and Ryan survive the helicopter explosion?” James asked.

“I’m not really sure how they did that, they walked away from it like nothing ever happened,” Wayne said.

“And why didn’t Little Darrel get mechanical legs? Like Juice’s mechanical arms?” Kate asked.

“Tyson and Ryan didn’t have any made at the time. They started making mechanical appendages a long time after Little Darrel lost his legs,” Wayne explained.

“Oh, I see,” Kate said.

“What about the Itches, how did they make it out of the prison?” James asked.

“The same way everybody else made it out, once Juice it started crumbling, everybody found their way out,” Wayne replied.

"So when do you think we'll fight Kronos?" James asked.

"I'm not sure, but I have a feeling that it will happen very soon," Wayne said.

"How did you guys learn all the names of the Skars and the Kuts?" Kate asked, as she looked at the others.

"Well, we battled them for years, decades. We did a lot of spying on them," Juice said.

Wayne, Juice and the Darrel bothers' father, has been telling this story to James and Kate all night long. Wayne's image was in the clouds. Down below, the Skratches were sitting around a bonfire in front of Juice's house, listening to him. All day they had been rebuilding the city, but haven't made much progress yet.

"Juice, my son, Kronos is near. I give you the power of strength, and invincibility. And this other gift…they are also invincible, sorry it took me so long."

Wayne said. His image disappeared. Then, Lola and Lilly came up behind them.

Lola and Lilly were riding on the dragon from Juice's hallucination.

Lola climbed off of the dragon and walked straight up to Juice. Juice gasped at the sight of her. He shot up off of his log, and hugged her.

"LOLA!! YOU'RE ALIVE!!" he shouted, "And that dragon…"

"Yeah, I named her Zayda," Lola said.

Wayne came back as an image in the clouds again, "You're welcome, son. Lola and Lilly are very important to your battle with the Titans. Big Darrel is the chosen one, James and Kate are also important, and you Juice, you must be the one to carry on my legacy, make it *your* legacy. You must ride like the wind, fight proud, my son!"

.

.

.
.
.
.
.
.
.
.

XXIV

Wayne's image disappeared again, but then reappeared as a normal person. He sat down next to Juice on a log. Hephaestus, God of fire and blacksmiths, walked up behind him, and sat down next to Ryan and Tyson.

"Ryan and Tyson, I should have told

you sooner… I am your father," Hephaestus said.

"What?"

"I am your father?"

"You mean…we're brothers?" Ryan asked.

"Yes, you and Tyson are brothers," Hephaestus replied.

"That explains how you can translate Greek writing Ryan, and that's how we survived the helicopter explosion, and the prison caving in on us…but who is our mom?" Tyson asked.

"Her name was Marylyn, she died just after you were born."

"So you left us without a mom, without any support at all," Tyson said angrily.

"It wasn't my choice! Zeus has this ridiculous rule about the Gods and their children with mortals."

"Oh…that's right, I forgot about that," Tyson said.

"You know I wouldn't have let you

die."

"Yeah, we know," they said at the same time.

"Wait a minute, what about that time in the supermarket when you told me and Darrel about the family that wasn't home when you went there?" Juice asked them.

"Well, the truth is, neither one of us ever had a family. We found each other at a shop that we believed to be Ryan's mom's. We sort of raised each other there," Tyson said.

Wayne started another story…

Remember when Juice went down the cliff side using the wench on the truck? Well after that, Little Darrel, the baby, Ryan, and Tyson went back to the city. They went to Ryan's mom's shop, which you now know that it's actually Tyson's mom as well, and headed down stairs. There, they found a secret passage way. They never knew about the passage way for their entire life. Tyson was just goofing around with the piano. He hit a few random notes and suddenly a door opened up in the floor. Beyond that door, was a set of stairs that led to a long tunnel. They found all of the Skratches and the Itches down there.

You see, I Hephaestus, built all of these passageways in these homes to keep the people safe from the Skars and Kuts. The passages connected between most of the houses and buildings. Sort of like a labyrinth, but not as confusing.

There is also a secret room full of weapons down there. Ryan and Tyson found it, and gathered up some weapons. Ryan picked up a twelve gauge, double barrel shotgun, and Tyson grabbed a high powered rifle.

With their new guns, they headed back to the Skar's village to look for Juice, but they couldn't find him anywhere.

Little Darrel stayed down in the tunnels and watched over his baby brother.

While Ryan and Tyson continued to search for Juice, they found a Skar. The giant red monster spotted them instantly and tried to stomp on them. Ryan rolled out of the way of the left foot, and Tyson dived backwards out of the way of the right foot. As Tyson was diving backwards, he took his rifle and shot up at the giant's face, but missed. Ryan was shooting his shotgun at the Skar's knees. Tyson stood up and joined in on the knee shootings. Angrily, the red monster kicked them both into nearby trees. Ryan and Tyson stood back up and continued shooting the knees. Finally, the Skar couldn't bare the pain anymore, and crumbled face first into the ground. The giant wasn't done yet though, he grabbed them both in his hands, and slammed them into the ground. Then he dragged them, along with his self to a cliff side.

"I'm taking you to my leader for a special feast," said the giant.

Ryan and Tyson slipped away as

soon as he said that, and they jumped on his back. They aimed their guns at the back of his head, and fired. The Skar was dead, and they threw him off of the cliff.

Another giant was down below, "NO! How dare you kill one of mine! How dare you go against me, the great giant they call Blade, King of the Skars! You will die for that, and you'll be on my dinner plate tonight!"

Ryan and Tyson ran away. Blade was throwing trees at them from behind. They ducked and dodged several trees until they came to a smaller Cliffside and jumped off of it. They ran all the way back to Ryan's mom's secret machine shop. Ryan never knew about his mom, but he knew that this was her workshop. Tyson didn't have a clue who his mom at the time either.

The shop was big enough to fit several eighteen wheelers in it, at least ten or more.

"We gotsta build a weapon, like a

big rig with guns on it," Ryan suggested.

"Or several trucks with guns on em, and a big helimacopter for us!" Tyson said.

"Ooh, I like that idea," Ryan said.

Wayne stopped the story there.

Hephaestus looked at Ryan and Tyson, "These two got the gift of their mechanical skills from me. That shop is where they built several big rigs with guns, and that helicopter. It took them sixteen years to build it all. They built that helicopter first. They used it to go hunting all the time. I don't know where Ryan got his crazyness from, but one day, he was hanging from the chopper as Tyson was flying it around. Ryan picked up a trom and threw it at a gort. Then he took another trom and threw it at a moothrob. They gathered up all three animals and had enough food to last them for a whole year."

“That was fun!” Ryan chuckled.

“Ryan, Tyson, I have something important to tell you guys. There is a quest that you guys must go on. I will be giving you the power of fire, so that you can withstand the temperatures on the planet Burx. Someday you will have to go there. I will tell you more about it later.

.

.

.

.

XXV

Zeus showed up.

“James, Kate, I have come to give you powers that will help you when the Titans get here. James, you get the power of electricity. Kate, you will have control of the wind,” Zeus said, then he turned to the others, “Frank, Tank, you will hold some of the same powers as the Darrel brothers, just the power of persuasion during war. Big Darrel, you are the chosen one. Juice, with immortality, you will be able to carry on your father’s legacy, and kill Kronos. Lola and Lilly, you two will also be invincible.”

“Wait a minute, how come everybody but me, Frank, and Tank get all the good powers? What am I supposed to do with my peg legs when I go to fight one of the Titan’s? And what about Daisy!! Juice get‘s Lola back but Daisy is gone! This is NOT fair!” Little Darrel complained.

“Hephaestus, will you build him a set of mechanical legs? Make it so they give him the ability to run up to sixty miles per hour. And I will try to bring Daisy back, but not today," Zeus said.

"What about me and my brother!?" Frank snapped.

"Ah, Frank, well, you and your brother deserve powers too. Especially sense your mother Paula died, and you had to raise Tank by yourself," Zeus said, "I give you both the power of incredible strength. And for the rest of you, actually this includes everybody, for warriors everywhere, raise your hands up to the air, you're warriors, warriors of this world. Thunder from the sky, sworn to fight and die, warriors of this world. Stand proud, with glory, and unity, hail, hail, hail."

.

.

.

.

.

.

.

.

.
.
.
.
.

Skratches

book three

Juice's Legacy

Coming Soon!

.
.
.
.
.
.
.
.
.
.
.
.
.
.

.
.
.

Glossary

Planets in the Universe of Olympus

Mechta: The fourth planet from Apollo. The land Planet.

Tuberok: The third planet from Apollo. The labyrinth planet, or the planet of tunnels.

Koalm: The second planet from Apollo. The water planet.

Burx: The closest planet to Apollo. It is so close that its surface is burnt to a crisp.

Apollo: The sun God, the Skratches call their sun Apollo.

Gods

Zeus - God of the sky, King of Kings. Son of Kronos and Rhea.

Poseidon - God of the Sea, father of the Sharkans, Cyclops, and many demi-gods. Zeus's brother.
Hades - God of the Underworld. Zeus's brother.
Hera - Goddess of Marriage, and Zeus's wife.
Ares - God of War, the father of Wayne.
Aphrodite - Goddess of Love, Ares' wife, mother of Wayne.
Hephaestus - God of fire and blacksmiths, father of Ryan and Tyson.
Dionysius - God of wine.
Hermes - God of messaging.
Athena - Goddess of Wisdom.
Apollo - the Sun God.
Artemis - Goddess of the Hunt.
Hestia - Goddess of the Hearth.
Demeter - Goddess of Agriculture.

I. Mechta

A. Clans on Mechta

Skratches: Juice, Little Darrel, Big Darrel; sons of the minor God Wayne, and his mortal Skratch wife, Carol. Frank, and Tank; sons of Paula, and nephews of Wayne and Carol. Ryan, and Tyson; Sons of Marylyn and the fire god, Hephaestus.

They are friendly. They are white/Caucasian skinned, with battle wounds. They come in many sizes from three feet, to ten feet.

Itches: Sledge, Hammer, Molly, Elizabeth, Max, Dominique, and Daisy.

These are allies of the Skratches, they look similar to the Skratches but with green skin.

Skars: Flame, Blaze, Slash, and Gash.

These are enemies of the Skratches and the Itches. They are all over thirty feet tall, with red skin, and they are covered with scars.

Kuts: Blade, Ax, Machete, Dagger, and Razor.

These are allies to the Skars. They are the same size as average humans. They are skeleton warriors that can turn into anyone's shadow and suffocate them. They have tails in the middle of their backs that can be used to hook on to something and hang or swing. They have lights in their foreheads, and they have tribal designs engraved into their bones.

Stitches: Dr. Bit, Dr. Bolt, Dr. Screw, and Dr. Nut. These are the only doctors on planet Mechta.

Mech-Skratches: Ryan and Tyson.

The only mechanics on the planet. They are also the blacksmiths.

B. Beer of Mechta

Krog: Beer.

Krog Light: Light beer.

C. Animals of Mechta

Gort: A two headed

deer/elk/bear/gorilla/tiger on planet Mechta. It has one head that is an a bear with elk horns, with saber-teeth. The other head is a normal deer with no horns(not a doe). It has the butt and legs of a gorilla, and the back of a grizzly bear.

Bealx: A type of badger on planet Mechta.

Moothrob: A type of cow on planet Mechta.

Dakovy: A type of monkey on planet Mechta.

Jamuk: A type of chipmunk on planet Mechta.

Zip: A type of small bird on planet Mechta.

Falvon: A type of large bird on planet Mechta.

Trom: A type of alligator on planet Mechta. It has the body of an alligator, the head of a T-Rex, a fin with spikes, teeth that curve, and a tail full of electricity.

Salawob: A type of frog on planet Mechta.
Warmot: A type of pig on planet Mechta.

D. Bugs of Mechta

Queep: A type of mosquito on planet Mechta.
Erak: A type of spider on planet Mechta.
Liak: A type of beetle on planet Mechta.
Skwig: A type of worm on planet Mechta.

Skratch words

Conflusteraboobermakated: (*cun-flust-er-a-boober-ma-kated.)* - Flustered and confused at the same time.
Hoobydoowhaty: (*who-bee-do-what-ee.)* - What did you say?

Hoobydoowhachyacaller: (or hoobydoowhachyacaller***s***) (*who-be-do-wuch-ya-call-er.)* - Something that someone can't think of what to call it, or what its name is.
Whatchahowdicky: (*wut-chuh-how-dicky)* - Another word for hoobydoowhachyacaller.
Thingamajig: Thingamajig.
Ottawanna: You might want to.
Idoewanna: I don't want to.
Idoowanna: I *do* want to.
Hafsta: Has to, or have to.
Gotsta: Got to.
Wantsta: Want to, or wants to.
Suh-um or Sumthin: Something.
Meechya: Meet you. (It's nice to meechya.)
Widda: with the.
Widja: with you.
Udder: Other.
Fer: For.
Wut: What.
Werd: Word.

Dat: That.
Dare: There.
Dis: This.
Da: The.
Dey: They.
Ta: To.
Thang: Thing.
Cun: Can.
Cud: Could.
Cuz: Because.
Didja: Did ya, or did you. (What *did you* do? Or, What *didja* do?)
Getchya: Get ya, or get you. (I'm here to getchya outta here. Or, I'm here to get you out of here.)
Idunno: I don't know.
Er: This word has many uses. It can be used to replace the words 'her', and 'or'. They use the word to replace the word her, in terms that they label many objects as females, mostly their vehicles. (I drove **er** up to the mountains. - in this sentence the Skratch is labeling the vehicle as a female.) (It looks like something **er** other.

- in this sentence, it is being used to replace the word ‘or’. This word can also be used when someone is thinking, for example: **Er**…um…Idunno wut da hoobydoowhachyacaller is supposed ta do. Da dang thang gots me all conflusteraboobermakated.

Greek letter	Letter name	English
Αα	Alpha	Aa
Ββ	Beta	Bb
Γγ	Gamma	Gg
Δδ	Delta	Dd
Εε	Epsilon	Ee
Ζζ	Zeta	Zz
Ηη	Eta	Hh
Θθ	Theta	TH th
Ιι	Iota	Ii
Κκ	Kappa	Kk
Λλ	Lambda	Ll
Μμ	Mu	Mm
Νν	Nu	Nn
Ξξ	Xi	Xx

Oo	Omicron	Oo	
Ππ	Pi	Pp	
Ρρ	Rho	Rr	
Σσ	Sigma	Ss	
Ττ	Tau	Tt	
Υυ	Upsilon	Uu	
Φφ	Phi	PH ph	
Χχ	Chi	CH ch	
Ψψ	Psi	PS ps	
Ωω	Omega	Ww	

Special thanks to : Ryan Spann, for giving me the idea for this book, and drawing up some of the characters and creatures.

&

Tyson Leonard, for giving me more ideas for this book.

.
.
.
.
.
.
.
.
.

Praise for more
Justin Robertson Books!

The Eyes of a Demon & The Eyes of a Demon II

The Eyes of a Demon - is also available in

eBook format, download it at the iBookstore or on Nook.

And…

***Skratches* book one.**

Available at www.lulu.com

&

www.amazon.com

www.ingramcontent.com/pod-product-compliance
Ingram Content Group UK Ltd.
Pitfield, Milton Keynes, MK11 3LW, UK
UKHW020129250726
13967UKWH00002B/552